BRAVE
RED,
SMART
FROG

Brave Red, Smart Frog

A New Book of Old Tales

Emily Jenkins

illustrated by Rohan Daniel Eason

Candlewick Press

Text copyright © 2017 by Emily Jenkins
Illustrations copyright © 2017 by Rohan Daniel Eason

First edition 2017

Library of Congress Catalog Card Number pending
ISBN 978-0-7636-6558-6

17 18 19 20 21 22 TLF 10 9 8 7 6 5 4 3 2 1

Printed in Dongguan, Guangdong, China

This book was typeset in Hightower.
The illustrations were done in watercolor and ink.

Candlewick Press
99 Dover Street
Somerville, Massachusetts 02144

visit us at www.candlewick.com

For my mother
E. J.

For my darling honey badger, Iris
R. D. E.

CONTENTS

SNOW
WHITE

THERE WAS ONCE a frozen forest, cold as cold ever was. Snow blanketed the ground. The frost sparkled. The streams were iced, the bushes bare. The paths were so narrow, no horse could walk through.

No woodcutters ever chopped anything down. People from nearby towns believed that vengeful sprites lived in the trees. They said witches lived in the winter wood, as well — some with cold hearts, and others with hot ovens and ugly appetites — and also dwarves, immune to the cold and sheltering in tiny houses made of stones.

On one side of this frozen forest stood a castle. In it lived a queen who was unhappy. She was a warm person, a bright person. Her husband was chilly and dull. It had been a mistake to marry him. When their first and only daughter was born, the king named the baby Snow White. The queen would have preferred a name like Tulip or Sunshine.

It was not long after Snow White's birth that our poor, warm queen caught a cold. It worsened and she died of it. Soon after that, the king married again. His new wife had walked out of the winter forest one day and charmed him with beauty like an icicle — sharp and slippery. She called herself January, and when she moved into the castle, she brought along nothing but an enchanted mirror.

This new queen felt invisible without a reflection of herself nearby. She spent hours staring into the mirror, touching her beautiful face, just to be certain she really existed. Every so often, she asked a question:

Mirror, mirror, on the wall,
Who is fairest of them all?

And each time, the mirror answered what January wished to hear:

You deserve an answer true,
There's no one here, so fair as you.

And January was happy — or, at least, pleased enough with her lot.

Snow White didn't bother with mirrors. She was warm and bright like her mother had been. Since the cooks and tailors of the castle were her only companions, she kept herself busy learning to cook and sew. As she grew older, she got even warmer and brighter, and by the time she was a young woman, Snow White was the sort of person who made you smile just to look at her.

There was beauty in her character.

By now, January was not so young as she once was. There were cracks on her face and a softness in her jaw. Some people find cracks and softness lovely, but January wanted the mirror to show the face she had seen long ago, a face of smooth and shining ice.

Mirror, mirror, on the wall,
Who is fairest of them all?

When she asked, the mirror had always replied:

You deserve an answer true,
There's no one here so fair as you.

That is, until one fateful day. It said:

You will not like my answer true:
Snow White is twice as fair as you.

Was it true? There are so many ways to measure beauty, and so many ways to enchant a mirror. We cannot know.

What matters is that January believed it. She gazed into the glass, peering at her face.

All she saw were cracks.

And that softness in her jaw.

January ordered the castle huntsman to bring Snow White into the frozen forest. When they were far from home, he was to kill her and cut out the warm, bright heart that beat in her chest.

January planned to eat it.

Yes, to eat the heart.

She believed it would restore her beauty.

THE HUNTSMAN was a kind man, but he followed orders. He took Snow White by the wrist and dragged her toward the trees.

Snow White fought, but the huntsman held fast.

She screamed and bit and kicked, but the huntsman held fast.

Finally, she begged. He held fast still.

He dragged Snow White along the narrow paths of the frozen forest into the dark.

But then, when they were far from home, he let her go. He would cut out a wolf's heart, he told her, and bring that to the queen instead.

Snow White thanked him.

He left her alone.

The bare branches of the trees clicked across one another.

Snow White shivered and crossed her arms around her body.

She could feel the cold through the soles of her boots.

She began to walk, and the eyes of hungry creatures followed her, but luck was on her side. It was only minutes before she came upon a tiny house built of stones. She stepped inside without knocking and shut the door behind her.

Inside, the ceiling was so low, Snow White could only just stand up. "Hello, is anyone home?"

There was no answer.

"Hello?"

Her eyes adjusted to the dark. She was in a kitchen. Burned pots and scorched pans sat on the counters. Stacks of dirty plates were piled on the table. A smell of singed meat and overboiled cabbage hung in the air. In the living room, dust and spilled sugar covered the tables. In the bedroom, Snow White found seven tiny beds, all with the bedclothes crumpled at the bottom. Tiny slippers and worn pairs of pajamas littered the floor.

The bathroom was too unpleasant to describe.

She rested and warmed herself, and waited for the owners to return home.

No one came. A storm began to blow outside.

With nothing else to do, Snow White cleaned the kitchen. And then the living room. The bedroom, and finally the bathroom. She mended the holes in the pajamas with a bolt of cloth she found in a closet. She roasted a joint of meat and cooked up a cabbage, one without burning and the other without overboiling. She was just pulling the meat from the oven when seven dwarves rushed inside. The snow stormed in behind them until they shut the door.

They were all men.

Very small and squat, only so high as Snow White's knees. They wore no coats, no hats, no winter gear at all.

"Who's the tall one?"

"What's she doing here?"

"Is she a witch?"

"She won't tell you if she is."

"Why is it clean?"

"She cleaned it, noodle."

"Why would she clean it?"

"Humans like clean."

"Witches like clean, too."

"What smells good?"

"The witch cooked."

"She's not a witch."

"She cooked our meat."

"She cooked our cabbage."

"Witches cook."

"Don't eat their food."

"She's not a witch."

"How can you tell?"

"I feel it in the bones."

"Stop it with your bones."

"The bones don't lie."

"Shut it, you."

"She's not a witch."

The other six dwarves must have believed the one who felt it in the bones, for they all took off their boots and walked into the kitchen in sock feet. They said nothing but sat down at the table, each grabbing a fork and plate on the way.

Snow White looked at the dwarves.

The dwarves looked at Snow White.

Then one of them stood up. Moving slowly, he dragged an armchair from the living room over to the kitchen table. "Sit down," he said. "And eat with us."

THAT IS HOW Snow White came to live with the seven dwarves of the frozen forest. They were strange little men, not exactly human. They were rotten cooks but good hunters, and kept stores of potatoes, cabbages, and carrots in a shed out at the back of their tiny stone house. They didn't mind the cold, couldn't read, argued constantly, and spent their days mining coal from deep below a mountain some miles away.

Snow White didn't tell them where she'd come from. It was too sad for her to talk about. Instead she made their house warmer and brighter, keeping it clean and teaching them how to cook so that things didn't burn or get overboiled. The eight of them lived like that together for some weeks. Snow White learned their names and darned their socks. The house was filled with laughter and friendship.

Back in the castle, the king did not even notice his daughter was gone. January had eaten the wolf's heart and was happy again — or, at least, pleased enough with her lot. That is, until the day she thought to ask again:

> *Mirror, mirror, on the wall,*
> *Who is fairest of them all?*

And the mirror replied:

> *You will not like my answer true:*
> *Snow White is still more fair than you.*

At this, January knew the huntsman had deceived her.

IT WAS NOT HARD for her to guess where Snow White had found shelter. January knew the forest well.

She went to the marketplace and bought a basket of red apples. Each one she rubbed with poison. Then she disguised herself with a hooded cloak and walked quickly into the winter woods.

The dwarves were working at the mine.

Snow White was home alone.

She hadn't eaten fruit in several weeks.

She hadn't left the stone house, so cold was the forest.

When the apple-seller knocked on the door of the stone house, Snow White wrapped herself in a blanket and answered the door.

"Sweet apples, fresh apples," croaked January.

"I am sorry. I have no money," Snow White told the hooded figure.

"You could make a pie," said the seller, holding up a shiny red apple.

Snow White would love a pie. The house would fill with the smell of warm fruit and sugar.

"I can't," she answered. "I have nothing to give."

"Take one for yourself, then," said the seller. "To eat. A gift."

"Thank you." Snow White took the apple and bit into it gladly. "Won't you come inside to warm yourself?"

"Oh, I'm not cold," the apple-seller said, and Snow White paused.

Not cold.

How could that be?

Any true human would be freezing.

She thought no more. Asked no questions. The poison had begun to work. Snow White collapsed lifeless in the doorway.

January threw off her cloak and pulled a knife. She would have the heart, she would. She would eat it and regain her beauty.

Knife drawn, she bent over Snow White . . . but was stopped by the sound of the seven dwarves, shouting and running at her, waving picks and mining lamps.

"Witch!" they yelled.

"Witch for sure!"

"I feel it in the bones!"

The dwarves chased January through the forest, swinging their axes and hurling stones.

She ran. And ran.

But not fast enough.

It was a bloody, bloody day.

At the end of it, January was dead.

When the dwarves returned to the stone house, Snow White seemed lifeless, but she was not cold.

Her skin was warm, though she did not breathe. Her face was pink, though her eyelids did not move.

"She's choked."

"She hasn't."

"She's poisoned."

"She isn't."

"She's magicked."

"Oh, no."

"She's gone and dead forever."

"She's alive, I tell you. I feel it in the bones."

"I think she needs sunlight."

"I think she needs warmth."

"Out of the winter."

"Yes, into the spring."

In the end, the seven dwarves carried Snow White out of the frozen forest and onto a hillside far from her father's castle. One of their number remained, keeping watch from behind a rock, and they left her lying there, hoping that the warm bright sun would work its magic.

An hour or so later, a prince rode by on horseback. He was a kind person: jolly and strong and fond of music and good things to eat. This prince, whose name was Beacon, saw Snow White lying on the hillside. The sun had warmed her, and she seemed not dead, but sweetly asleep.

He stopped his horse and watched her breathing.

Her eyelids fluttered.

Prince Beacon liked Snow White's face for its courage and kindness, and he was also a curious fellow who liked most pretty girls and all new adventures.

And so, he woke her up.

Now, some kisses break enchantments.

And other kisses begin them.

Beacon's kiss was the second kind, not the first. Snow White woke to bright sunshine and a friendly face.

A new life was what she needed. Now, with seven new friends and an eighth to love, there was finally one ahead of her.

THE
FROG PRINCE

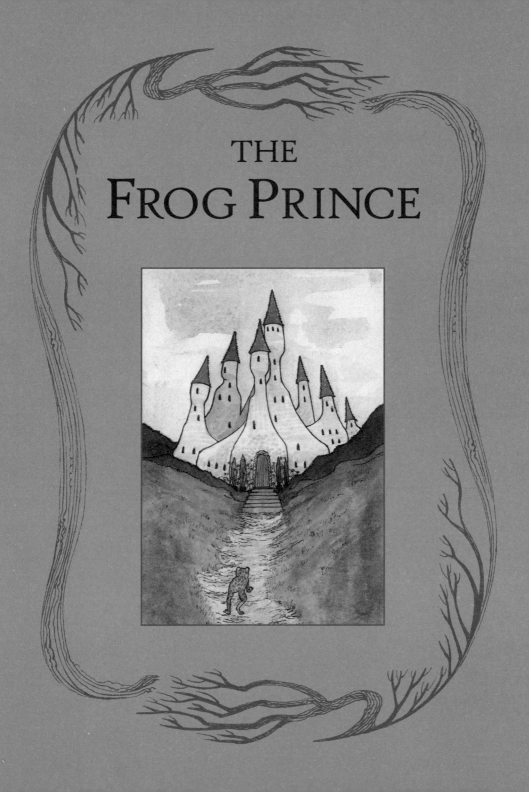

THERE WAS ONCE A PRINCESS, young enough to play with toys but old enough to think about marriage. This is not a long period in a person's life, and it makes her feel uncomfortable. She is not a child but not all the way a grown-up, either.

This princess, Crystal, was beautiful to most people's way of thinking—except for those people who see beauty in character. In character, she was flawed.

She had too many pretty dresses.

Too many pairs of shoes.

She had too many curls in her hair, too many roses

in her cheeks, too many chocolates before dinner, too many ladies-in-waiting instead of friends.

Even worse, Crystal had too few occupations and too few real conversations. The ladies-in-waiting agreed with whatever she said. They did whatever she wanted to do. "Yes, Princess," "Of course, Princess," and "You know best, Princess," all day long. Crystal was fretful and spoiled, spiteful and desperately lonely.

One day, tired of trying on clothes and eating chocolates, Crystal took her favorite golden ball out to the castle grounds. She could have forced some member of the castle staff to play with her, but a game never feels the same when people are paid to play it with you.

The golden ball had been a gift from her mother when she was young. Her mother was dead, and Crystal missed her dearly.

This day, Crystal walked to the top of a hill and tossed the ball high, admiring its golden shine against the blue sky before she caught it again. On the third toss, however, she missed her catch, and the ball bounced down the hill at high speed.

Crystal chased it.

The ball bounced down through the rose garden and then through the vegetable garden at the back of the castle kitchen. Then it kept on downhill, shining merrily, until it landed in the well at the base of an herb garden.

Out of breath, the princess leaned over and looked at the water.

It was very, very deep.

She lowered the bucket into the well and raised it again, hoping to retrieve the ball.

Only water.

She lowered it again, and again, and again.

Only water.

Now, in the way of princesses who are not used to solving their own problems, and of girls who have lost their mothers, and of girls who are young enough to play with toys but old enough to think about marriage, Crystal sobbed bitterly.

She leaned her cheek against the cold stone of the well. "I would give anything if only I could have my ball back."

"Anything?"

A frog had spoken. It was moss green and as big as Crystal's head. Its eyes goggled out of its body. Its strange dry lips were curled in something that might have been a smile. In other words, the frog was of surpassing ugliness to everyone. That is, except for those who see beauty in character.

Crystal jumped back in surprise and disgust. "Where did you come from?"

"From the well," answered the frog. "Did I scare you?"

"No."

"I think I did."

"No."

"You jumped back."

"You did not scare me, slimy thing."

The frog drew itself up. "I'm not slimy. Touch me. You'll see."

"No!"

"Try it."

"I will not."

"I'm dry. Just use one little finger you don't much care about."

"Never, not ever."

"Your loss," said the frog. "Why should I care if a dairy maid feels my skin?"

"I'm not a dairy maid."

"Pardon me," said the frog. "A kitchen maid."

"Sure as sure, I am the princess."

"Sure as sure, nothing," said the frog. "Here you are in the herb garden. The bottom of your dress is covered in mud, and your face is puffy. I'm no noodle. A princess is clean and doesn't let her nose run without finding a handkerchief."

There was nothing Crystal could say to that. She dug in her pocket, found a handkerchief, and wiped her nose. "I lost my ball down the well," she told the frog. "I'll give anything to get it back."

"Anything?"

"Anything." Crystal nodded.

"Well, what you have to give is considerable, if you really are the princess," said the frog.

"I am the princess."

"Maybe."

She flicked him with her finger. "I am! You know it."

"Only maybe."

She flicked him again.

"You touched me," croaked the frog gleefully. "You said never, not ever, and still you touched me."

"Only to flick you," said Crystal.

The frog turned around and hopped along the edge of the well. "You don't want me to get your ball for you, then."

"But I do!" Crystal followed him. "Pretty please, my warty friend, get it for me. I promise I'll reward you however you please."

The frog disappeared down the well in a series of long hops, his suckered feet sticking to the stone.

After some time, he reappeared, holding the golden ball in his lipless mouth.

"You've slimed it," said the princess, taking it from him.

Then she ran away laughing, with never a thought of keeping her promise.

THAT NIGHT, Crystal had dinner with her father, the king. As usual, they sat at either end of a long table in an enormous hall. They ate from silver plates and drank from golden goblets.

Crystal told her father about the ball and the frog, but after that, there wasn't much to say.

There never was.

After the servants cleared the plates and set down dessert of strawberries and cake, a rap sounded at the door that opened on the kitchen garden.

Crystal went to it and there sat the frog, round as a doughnut and ten times the size. He hopped into the dining hall and over to the princess's chair. "Lift me up."

"I'm not lifting you up. You came to dinner uninvited."

"I did you a kindness. You owe me a reward. You left without paying it," said the frog. "Lift me up."

Crystal reached down and grabbed the dry but definitely warty frog underneath the belly. She hoisted him up and set him on the table. "This is the frog who helped me get my ball back," she explained to her father. "He's come to claim his reward."

"If you promised a reward, you must pay it," said the king. "What does he want?"

"I want only this," said the frog to Crystal. "To

eat with you at your table and to sleep with you on your pillow."

"Oh, no."

"Oh, yes."

"Ask for diamonds."

"What would I do with diamonds?"

"Then ask for riches."

"What would I do with riches?"

"Then ask for a pond. A pond with lily pads, and a thousand thanks," said Crystal.

"I do not want a pond," said the frog. "I want company."

"You do not."

"I do."

"If he will not take diamonds or riches or a pond, then you must pay the reward he asks," said the king.

"You just want to slime up my table," said Crystal to the frog. "You want to get your horrendous froggy tongue all over my slice of cake."

"A little cake would be nice, thank you," said the frog. "You can put some here, in that saucer for me. Then you won't get my frog germs."

"I still have to look at you," said Crystal, but she

cut a generous slice of the cake, put it on the saucer, and added several strawberries.

The frog shoved his face into the cake and ate everything with enthusiasm, even the little green leaves of the strawberries. Crystal, who was used to formal table manners, found herself smiling. They talked about stories she'd read and adventures he'd had, about cake and music and birdsongs.

That night, the frog slept on Crystal's pillow.

"Stop breathing," said she. "You're breathing too loud."

"You stop breathing."

"No, you."

"No, you."

"You smell like a frog," she complained.

"You smell like a human," he complained right back, "and your hair takes up too much room on the pillow."

"At least I'm not bald and warty."

"I'm good-looking to other frogs," said the frog. "Other frogs find me very attractive."

"Why are you even here, then? Why would you want to be here with me?"

"It's chilly out," said the frog. "There's nobody to talk to."

And with that, the two of them went to sleep.

THE NEXT MORNING when Crystal awoke, the frog was nowhere to be found. She spent the day with her ladies-in-waiting, trying on dresses, being measured for dresses, trying on jewels and slippers and hats. It was "Yes, Princess," "Of course, Princess," and "You know best, Princess," all day long.

When she arrived in the grand hall for dinner with her father, Crystal looked eagerly for the frog.

He was not there.

"You have paid your debt to him," said the king, "so he has gone back to his mudhole."

At this, the princess felt heavy and sorry for herself. The meat tasted like cardboard. The roasted apples were sour, the potatoes dry and mealy. She thought of the frog, with cake on his bloated froggy face, and felt that dinner with her father was even duller than a day with her ladies-in-waiting.

She jumped as soon as she heard a knock at the door, and when she saw the frog upon the doorstep, she picked him up gleefully and kissed him on his dry, bald, warty, froggy head, she was so very glad to see him.

Now, some kisses break enchantments.

And other kisses begin them.

Crystal's kiss was the first kind, not the second. As soon as her lips touched the frog, he wrenched out of her hands — and before he hit the ground, he was transformed.

Before her stood a tall, broad-shouldered man, just a little older than herself, not froggy in the least, though his large warm eyes looked familiar. It was the frog himself, and Crystal felt both surprised and unsurprised, as if she had known there was magic of this sort at work all along.

"I want only this," he said. "To eat with you at your table and to sleep with you on your pillow."

"You just want to slime up my table," said Crystal. "You want to get your horrendous froggy tongue all over my slice of cake."

"I have a normal human tongue now," he said. "And while it's true I'm fond of cake, I'm fonder by far of you."

"Cheeky," scolded Crystal, but she smiled as she led the way to the table and offered him a chair. Cake was served; the two of them devoured it in big, joyful mouthfuls, and then asked for seconds. The young man told Crystal and her father his story.

Years ago, he had been prince of a neighboring kingdom. He had angered an ill-tempered witch, and she had punished him by turning him into a frog. A frog he had remained for a good long time, knowing that the only thing that could break his enchantment was true love's kiss — but never dreaming he would find it.

"You think I love you, then?" said Crystal. "We only met yesterday."

"I know you love me," said the prince, laughing. "If you didn't love me, I would still be a frog."

"Oh, all right, it's true, but don't gloat about it. It's disgusting," said the princess, putting her hand on his.

He stopped her mouth with a second kiss.

And after that, they married, and spent their hours talking and laughing and teasing each other, only quarreling now and then to keep the days from seeming dull.

THREE
WISHES

THERE WAS ONCE a woodcutter who lived near the edge of a frozen forest; a forest where it was always winter. Perhaps you know of it.

The woodcutter did not cut wood in that forest, because people in the towns nearby believed the trees were haunted by sprites who would take vengeance on anyone who cut down their homes. Therefore, each morning the woodcutter drove his cart and donkey several miles away to a sunny forest populated by bunnies and bluebirds. He cut down the trees there, instead.

He loved the bunnies. He loved the bluebirds. He loved the smell of fresh-cut wood and the feel of the ax in his hands. He loved his wife; he loved his children; he loved his soft-nosed, dear old donkey. His name was Twig, this woodcutter, and he was very happy in his life.

Then one day, the donkey died. It was very old.

After that, Twig became stupid with grief. True, it was only a donkey, but it had been his pet and helper for many years. And so, he did not cut wood.

Twig did not cut wood and he did not cut wood, and therefore he did not sell wood and he did not sell wood. Instead, he moped around the house, thinking about the donkey's soft nose and sweet, unquestioning nature.

Finally his wife, Butter — who made dinner, did the accounts, and looked after their four children — said to him, "Twig. You have got to sell wood. You're a woodcutter."

"I have no donkey to pull the cart," Twig answered.

"Why not buy a new donkey?"

"We are too poor. I have sold no wood for months on months. Our savings are gone."

"Why didn't you buy a new donkey when the old one died?"

"I was too sad. I loved our donkey."

"You must cut wood in the frozen forest, then," said Butter, "for it is nearby enough that you won't need the cart."

"The frozen forest?" Twig was frightened.

"If you do not cut wood, we will have nothing to eat in this house but boiled cabbage and fish heads."

And although he did not like boiled cabbage and fish heads any more than you do, Twig was frightened of the frozen forest and, still, he did not cut wood.

He did not cut wood and he did not cut wood, and he did not sell wood and he did not sell wood.

His children ate boiled cabbage and fish heads.

He and Butter ate boiled cabbage and fish heads.

And it was not long before the fish heads became too expensive, and they ate nothing but boiled cabbage, day in and day out.

One afternoon, after lunching on cabbage while looking at the sad, cabbage-sick faces of his four children, Twig could take it no more.

He shouldered his ax and pulled his wheelbarrow

from the shed. He kissed his wife and walked bravely into the forest.

The moment he set foot on the narrow path that went through the trees, Twig felt a chill. Only a few paces farther and he was shivering, his hands stiffening under his gloves, his ears turning pink with the cold.

The bare branches of the trees clicked across one another.

No bunnies scrabbled in the underbrush. No bluebirds chirped in the branches.

Twig could feel the cold through the soles of his boots.

He went on for some time until, deeper into the wood, the trees became thick enough to cut down. He chose one that was a good size for splitting and carting home. He raised his ax.

"Stop!"

At his ear was a tree sprite. She was the same ash-brown color as the tree he was preparing to chop, with an angry face and wings like winter leaves — rusty, crumpled, and papery.

"Don't cut my tree!" cried the sprite. "I beg you.

Don't leave me to the mercy of the wolves and the ravens. They are starving and have no mercy to spare. Without the tree to protect me, I'll be dead before nightfall."

"I am sorry," he said. "I have four hungry children to feed, a wife who isn't pleased with me, and a dear sweet donkey who is many months dead. I must cut wood to feed my family."

"Each tree in this forest protects a sprite," the creature explained. "You cannot cut wood here at all. You will kill us."

Twig thought of raising his ax, but found he could not do it. Instead, he nodded and prepared to go home, lifting the handles of the barrow and turning back along the path.

"Wait!" cried the sprite. "For your charity, I reward you with three wishes. What do you wish for?"

"Oh, I must consult my wife," replied Twig. "If she hasn't got a hand in choosing the wishes, she'll be even less pleased with me than she is now."

"The next three wishes you voice will come true," said the sprite. "And I'm very sorry about your donkey."

TWIG HURRIED HOME, but it was late in the evening when he arrived. The children were asleep, and Butter waited at the door.

"Where is the money?" she asked him.

"I have none."

"Then, where is the food? Surely you have sold the wood, spent the money, and brought us food?"

"I have not."

"Idiot!" she cried. "Where is the wood, then?"

Butter was not a cruel woman, but remember: she was very, very hungry.

"I did not cut wood," said Twig, and with that, Butter turned her back on him, stomped into the house, and busied herself sweeping the floor of the kitchen.

Twig followed. He explained to her about the frozen forest, the narrow path, the tree sprite who was frightened of wolves and ravens, and finally the three wishes. "I wanted to consult you before making a wish," he said.

"Stop it," snapped Butter. "I know there are no wishes. I know there was no sprite. You slept the day away while your children went hungry, and now you come home to me with a mouth full of lies."

"But it's true!" cried Twig. "Let me prove it! I wish we had a fat squashy sausage for our dinner."

And with that, a fat squashy sausage, warm and steaming slightly, appeared on the table.

"See?" said Twig.

"You wasted a wish on a sausage."

"But you like sausage," said Twig. "I picked sausage because I know you like it!"

"I'd like a larder full of food that would last us the winter," snapped Butter. "I'd like a cow that we could milk, or a garden we could tend. I'd like shoes for the children or a donkey to pull your cart again. I'd like a sack of money or ten years of good health or a husband with half a brain, which is more than the husband I've got. Wishing for a sausage," she sniffed. "No one but a child would wish for a sausage."

"I went in the forest like you wanted," said Twig.

"You're a great noodle," said his wife. "Mooning about that donkey for months upon end when your own children eat nothing but cabbage."

"Aw, come on, let's eat the sausage," said Twig. "It's such a fat squashy one."

"Don't touch it!" cried Butter. "If we eat it, we have to keep it. If we don't eat it, maybe there's a way we can undo the wish."

"I'm hungry." Twig reached out.

"No." Butter grabbed it. "It's a stupid sausage."

They each had one end and began pulling back and forth.

"Don't say *stupid sausage*. It did nothing to you," said Twig.

"Stupid, stupid sausage," said Butter.

"Well, then: I wish that stupid sausage was on the end of your stupid nose!" cried Twig.

As soon as he spoke those words, the sausage sprang to the end of Butter's nose and attached itself there, fat and squashy. When Butter turned her head, it flapped her on the shoulder. When she nodded, it bounced.

Twig laughed. He pointed. He felt pleased, the way one does when one has won an argument — until his wife, whom he really did adore, crumpled into a chair sobbing. The sausage shook as she wept.

"If we eat it now," said Twig, helpfully, "it'll look a lot better. It'll just be a little sausage stub on your nose. No one will hardly notice it!"

"I don't want a sausage stub on my nose," moaned Butter.

"We'll eat it right down," said Twig. "It'll be a very tiny sausage stub, I promise."

"I don't want a very tiny sausage stub, either."

"We'll use the last wish however you want. Do you think a cow is best? Or a donkey? Do you think we could get a donkey and a cow and maybe a pig all in one wish? Perhaps we could just say, 'An assortment of farm animals'!"

"I can't think with this sausage," sobbed Butter.

"Aw, come on, love," said Twig. "I'll still think you're pretty with a sausage stub. Really, I will. And I don't give three figs if the neighbors talk."

Butter thought for a long while. Finally she said, "I am lucky to have a husband who thinks I'm pretty with a sausage stub. And I am lucky to have a husband who doesn't give three figs if the neighbors talk."

"Thanks, my dear," said Twig. He kissed her on her nose, right next to the sausage. It smelled delicious.

"But I don't think I'm pretty, and I do care three figs if the neighbors talk," continued Butter. "I can't live with even the tiniest sausage stub, Twig. I truly cannot." And she began to cry again, crying for the cow and the donkey they would never have, for the cabbage-sick faces of the children and the unchoppable trees of the winter forest, for her sons' and daughters' worn-out shoes and the barren land behind their home that would never be a garden. She cried and cried, and Twig patted her back until at last he said:

"I wish the sausage off your nose."

In an instant it was back on the table.

Butter wiped her eyes and looked at it. "We are lucky it's still here," she said. "It might have gone entirely."

"That we are," said Twig.

And so they ate half of it for dinner and saved the rest for the children's breakfast. They laughed at each other's jokes and patted each other's arms and talked about what they would do the next day, and how they would work together.

TOADS
AND
PEARLS

THERE WAS ONCE a child whose mother died. The girl was mournful and sometimes lonely, but she did not turn bitter. In fact, she was sweet as cherries.

Along about the same time, there was another child whose father died. This girl was bitter as walnuts. She felt the world had wronged her and planned to punish it in return.

The father of the one and the mother of the other met and decided to marry. They shared money, meals, and a small home, living together for a short time in harmony.

However, one day the man encountered a hungry wolf.

That was the end of him.

He left behind the sweet girl, the bitter girl, and, bitterest of all, a woman who had lost two husbands in only two years.

The sweet one had the worst of it. Her stepmother and stepsister made her scrub the floors and wash the windows, beat the carpets and cook the meals. They made her do the dishes, wash the clothes, make the beds, and mend the holes in their stockings. They scolded her and hit her and told her she was worthless.

They themselves did very little. They had lost two men, the world was cruel, and they were far too unhappy to make dinner.

Cherry — the sweet one, that was her name — was as angry at those two as anyone could be. Who can blame her? Still, she managed to keep her temper most times and to enjoy the sun on a beautiful day, the taste of good cheese, the purr of a kitten.

Things went on in this unpleasant fashion until early one important morning, when Cherry went to get water from the well. It was a walk of some ten minutes, and as she turned home with her jug full, a crone appeared on the path. The woman's fingers were long. Her nose was hooked. She staggered and mumbled. She was dirty and her teeth rotted.

"May I have a drink of that water?" she asked. "I have no cup of my own."

Cherry was tired already. She knew her stepmother and stepsister would be impatient for the water she was carrying. The crone was unclean, even frightening. Cherry wanted to pull back, but instead she looked at the woman's face.

What did she see?

Need.

Cherry offered the jug.

The crone drank. When she finished, she said, "For your sweetness, I reward you with pearls."

Cherry laughed, it seemed so impossible, but as she laughed, her mouth filled with small spheres. They rolled gently off her lips and into her hand. Cherry looked down to see a pile of exquisite pearls.

When she looked up, the crone had disappeared.

AT HOME, her stepmother was furious. "Where is the water, stupid girl?"

Cherry flushed. She had forgotten to refill the jug. "I met a crone by the well," she answered, "and she blessed me somehow." As she spoke, pearls began rolling off her tongue. Pearl after pearl after pearl. They clattered to the floor and rolled across the boards.

Her stepsister, Walnut — that's what they called her — dropped to her knees to pick them up. "Are they real?"

"I don't know." More pearls hit the floor. Pearl after pearl after pearl.

"Disgusting. They're wet!"

"Sorry."

"Don't speak, then!"

"Sorry."

"Don't speak!"

Hand clamped over her mouth, Cherry sat down in a corner.

"She *should* speak, you noodle," cried the stepmother. "These pearls will be our fortune. Goodness knows we deserve it after all we've been through."

And so, Cherry spoke. She spoke of frivolities and forests, of wolves and moonlight, the past and the future. Pearls dropped from her lips with every sentence. You might think it would be uncomfortable, but instead it felt to Cherry as if she were saying exactly what she intended, the way you might feel when words roll off your tongue in shiny perfection. It felt surprising, but beautiful and satisfying.

The stepmother and Walnut knelt on the floor, scooping the pearls into a basket. Wet handful by wet handful, pearl after pearl after pearl.

"I love you," said the stepmother, "and perhaps I haven't told you as much as you might like to hear it. You, my Cherry, you are a beautiful girl with beautiful curls and beautiful pearls. I couldn't adore you more."

NEXT MORNING, Cherry set out to bring water from the well, but Walnut was standing outside. She smacked Cherry on the side of the head and took the jug out of her hands. "Don't you go again. I'm going."

Cherry stopped in surprise.

"The crone gave you pearls yesterday in exchange for water," said Walnut. "If you go again today, she'll give you something else, won't she? Rubies or emeralds or maybe diamonds."

Cherry shrugged.

"I've had a hard life," said Walnut. "I lost my father and then I lost my stepfather and we've got a poky little house and nothing fun ever happens. Anyone would feel sorry for me. Let me get the water today, and I'll come back with diamonds, just you wait and see."

Cherry left Walnut with the jug and went indoors silently.

AS WALNUT WALKED the path to the well, she stumbled and moped to make herself look as miserable as possible, but the crone was nowhere in sight.

Walnut filled the jug and began to carry it back, pausing often to sigh and stare at the sky. If the crone was hiding nearby, she would surely see how very unhappy poor Walnut was—and reward her suffering with jewels.

She was almost home when a small boy ran up behind her on the path. He was dirty and had green goop coming out his nose. "Oooh, could I have a drink of water?" he asked Walnut. "I have no cup."

"Not with that nose. Be off."

"What's wrong with my nose?"

"Go away."

"Come on," said the boy, wiping his snot on the back of his hand. "Be nice. I'm awful thirsty."

"Have you seen a crone nearby?" asked Walnut. "A crone who might be a fairy and takes pity on poor depressed girls like myself?"

"I haven't seen anyone. Please, may I have some water?" he repeated. "I have no cup. I am horrible dry in the mouth, lady."

"Get on away from me," said Walnut. "Germy little runt, you."

At that, the boy kicked her in the shin, making her drop the jug. It broke, and the water spilled out across the ground. "For your bitterness," he yelled, as he ran away laughing. "For your bitterness, I reward you with toads!"

"You're a toad, runt!" yelled Walnut, shaking her fist at him — but as she spoke, her mouth filled with slimy objects, each the size of your big toe. She spat them harshly into her hand. There were two brown toads and a green one wiggling on her palm.

"Disgusting!" she said. A large yellow toad formed in her mouth, forced its way out, and joined its fellows in her hand.

Walnut screamed and dropped the toads. As she did, four small red ones leaped from her tongue onto the wet ground, where they splashed happily in the puddle by the broken jug. Walnut stomped them angrily, but they were extremely fast, and even when she did manage to step on one, it popped back as if made from rubber.

Hand clamped over her mouth, Walnut ran home as fast as she could go, the eight toads hopping cheerily behind her.

Well, you can only imagine.

Walnut's mother insisted she tell the story of what had happened at the well, and with each word she spoke, Walnut produced another toad—the longer the word, the larger the beastie.

Soon the poky house was filled with toads. Toads in the sink, toads in the cooking pot, toads in the cups and saucers. Toads on shoulders and toes, toads on pillows and sponges, tiny toads in the curves of spoons. And, oh, the croaking and belching that filled the house!

Walnut stood on a chair and screamed, which only made sickly white toads the size of bread loaves force themselves from her mouth. The stepmother grabbed hold of an iron pot and began banging at toads right and left, but no matter what she did, no matter how hard she bashed them, they popped up again merrily.

Cherry opened all the doors and windows and tried to shoo the toads outside, but the longer Walnut screamed, the more they seemed to like it, and as many came back indoors as she could coax out.

"This is Cherry's fault!" cried the stepmother harshly. "If she had not lied about the crone, this never would have happened!" And she came at Cherry with the iron pot, looking to beat her with it.

Cherry was quick-footed and strong from all her

work, though. She dodged her stepmother and ran out the door. She ran for some time, past the outskirts of the nearest town, and then began to walk.

Then she changed direction and kept walking.

Cherry never wanted to go back to that house again.

She wanted to make a life for herself somewhere new.

She realized now that the crone had given her a great gift, indeed: independence. With pearls coming from her mouth, Cherry would never again be poor. She would never again need to live with people who were cruel to her, merely because those cruel people put a roof over her head.

She came to a town, rented a room, and paid in pearls.

RED RIDING HOOD

THERE WAS ONCE a forest; a strange forest, where it was always winter. You have heard of it before.

Nothing good to eat grew there. All the streams were frozen, and no fish ever swam in them. Almost no one lived there, either. Only some dwarves, tree sprites, an untold number of witches — and one or two humans who weren't suited to ordinary life.

As you might imagine, the animals of the frozen forest were very, very hungry.

Through the trees carved winding paths, too thin

and icy for horses to walk. And deep among the trees lay a locked house, built years ago by a man and a woman who had quarreled with their relatives and liked to live alone.

Now, the man was dead, and the woman was very old, indeed. We shall call her Grandmother, though she had not seen her daughter in a long, long time and had never met her granddaughter at all.

Where the wintery trees stopped, near a warm sunny meadow where horses roamed, lay another house. This house itself looked relieved — as if it had narrowly escaped being swallowed by the forest. In it lived a girl who was always called Red, because of the hooded red cloak she wore when she rode horses in the meadow.

One day, Red's mother received a letter, delivered by a dwarf. Grandmother, who lived in the locked house, deep in the wintery forest — Grandmother was ill. She longed to see her granddaughter. She wanted to gaze on the rosy cheeks and bright eyes of youth before she died.

Grandmother did not wish to see anyone else.

Indeed, she asked them not to come.

Red's mother baked corn cakes. A gift for Grandmother. An apology. A peacemaking.

When the cakes were ready, clouds were gathering in the sky. Red's mother asked her not to go. The frozen forest was dangerous enough without a storm. But Red would not hear of any more delay.

Grandmother wanted her; Grandmother was dying. She would go.

Mother drew her a map, to guide her through the dangerous woods, and Red walked into the dark.

The bare branches of the trees clicked across one another.

Red's cloak billowed out behind her.

Snow began to fall.

She had been walking for nearly an hour when the wind snatched the map from her hand. It flew into the clutches of an oak.

Could she climb and retrieve it?

No. The tree was coated in ice. Should she turn home?

No. She might never meet her grandmother.

"Are you lost?" The voice she heard was coated in honey. Red started and looked around.

There was no one there. No one she could see.

"I am not lost," she lied.

"Where are you going?" asked the voice.

Red made out two warm eyes, peering from behind a tree.

A wolf. Scrawny. Wet with snow and starving.

"My grandmother lives in this forest," Red told him. "She is expecting me."

"That is your grandmother, in the sugar house?"

"No."

"The stone house?"

"No."

"In the locked house, then?" asked the wolf.

"Yes," answered Red. "That must be her."

He trotted toward her like a dog and sniffed at the napkin covering the corn cakes.

"They're a gift," she said. "But take one. You look hungry." Red gave him a still-warm cake.

The wolf ate it in two bites. "You are very kind," he said. "May I have another?"

He was so hungry. Starving, even, but Red clutched her basket to her chest. "I am sorry, but you may not," she told him. "They are a gift for Grandmother. An apology. A peacemaking. She is weak and dying."

The wolf's eyes grew big. He licked his lips.

For the first time, Red was afraid.

But then he wagged his tail. "Thank you for the one cake, anyway. In return, I will tell you the shortest path to Grandmother's."

The wolf gave clear directions. Bear right, not left. Cross the frozen stream on the fallen tree. Bear left, not right.

All the while, Red was thinking: *I am so glad I found him. So glad I helped him. If not, for certain I'd be lost in this storm.*

All the while, the wolf was thinking: *the locked house is warm and full of good smells, but till this day, Grandmother was too smart to answer the scratch of a wolf at her door.*

Today, she is weak and dying. Today, as never before, she is expecting company. And I am so, so hungry, thought the wolf. *So very hungry.*

"Good-bye," said Red. "Thank you."

"Good-bye," said the wolf. "Travel safely."

He felt his fur prickle in disgust at what he knew he was about to do.

Red walked. Bearing right instead of left. Crossing the frozen stream. Bearing left instead of right. She kept her cloak tight about her as protection. The walk took nearly an hour, but because the snow fell so hard and fast, and because the wind blew loud and mean, she traveled safely. No other animals were hunting.

The wolf trotted through the trees only a short way. He knocked with a cold paw at the door of the locked house.

"Who is it?" Grandmother took a long time coming to the door.

"Granddaughter," said the wolf, altering his voice as best he could. "You expect me, don't you?"

"Red?"

"Yes. I've come to see you, Grandmother."

Grandmother unlocked the door.

The smell of potato soup reached the wolf.

The door opened inward, and he was upon her.

He swallowed her whole, then swallowed her soup and her bread and her ale.

He rummaged her closet and put on her clothes.

Red arrived walking slowly, head bowed against the wind. She tapped the door only to find it swing in at her touch.

"Grandmother," she called, entering. "It's Red. I've come with a basket of corn cakes."

No answer, but the bedroom door was open. "Grandmother?"

Red set the basket on the kitchen table and pushed forward. She had never met her grandmother. The figure before her was gnarled and frail, wrapped tightly in a robe and scarf.

"Grandmother?" Red said again as she approached. "Do you know me?"

"I know you," said the wolf.

"What big eyes you have," she said, her voice no louder than a whisper.

"The better to see you with, my dear. Come closer."

Red stepped. And stepped.

"What big ears you have," she said.

"The better to hear you with, my dear. Come closer, still."

It was her grandmother. It must be. Her grandmother had written and asked for Red, in her last days of life.

Red stepped. And stepped.

"What big teeth you have," she said, as she came to the bed.

And the wolf, though he hated himself, though he hated the frozen forest and what it had made of him, the wolf hated hunger even more.

"The better to eat you with, my dear," he said, and pounced.

He was so hungry, he swallowed Red whole.

It took only a moment. She didn't feel pain.

It was the wolf who felt pain, but he did not stop himself till the last of the bright red hood was down his throat.

Now with Grandmother, soup, bread, ale, and Red, the wolf should have been sated — but deep hunger can be like this: eating merely makes you want more.

He threw off the clothes and dragged his stuffed

body to the kitchen. As he ate the corn cakes, he knew he could be spied clearly through the window of the locked house.

But no one would see him, he thought. Hardly anyone came into the icy forest. And today, the sky was black with storms.

Still, someone did see the wolf.

A huntsman returning from a terrible errand stood outside the locked house, wondering if he might take shelter there from the cold. He knew full well that a wolf on a kitchen table is a dangerous, dangerous thing, and he was out to hunt a wolf, in any case.

The huntsman pushed the unlocked door open and discharged his rifle.

Blood spattered across Grandmother's tablecloth.

The wolf was hungry no more.

The huntsman shut the door against the cold. He rebuilt the fire. Then he took his knife and cut open the wolf. He needed the heart for his purposes.

Red was there. Inside the wolf. Alive and breathing.

Grandmother was there, too.

They two were there, embracing and laughing, even though they were strangers. They were safe and warm, and that was suddenly more than lucky enough in this world.

The snow piled high outside, and the three people were grateful for what they had, there in the locked house in the forest of winter.

Travel home would wait for another day.

THE
THREE GREAT
NOODLES

THERE WAS ONCE a farmhouse, and in it lived a vegetable farmer, a dairy farmer, and their daughter.

The three of them lived on a small farm near a sunny forest populated by bunnies and bluebirds. They raised turnips and sweet potatoes that fed them through the winter, and beans and tomatoes that fed them in the summer. They had a donkey to pull the cart and three cows that gave milk, which the mother turned to cheese and butter.

Eventually the daughter of this family was old enough to think about marriage. Her name was Amity.

A young man from town came courting Amity, after meeting her when she was selling her mother's cheese at market. His name was Blunt. He had been to school. He had a sharp mind and a kind heart, but something of a quick temper.

One day, Blunt and the family sat down to a meal in the farmhouse. They wanted wine, so Amity took a jug and went to fill it from the cask in the cellar.

As she turned the tap and let the wine flow, Amity looked up and saw an ax hanging from a hook above her head. She was tenderhearted, and the ax got her thinking. Amity thought and thought, and as she thought she began to cry.

Ten minutes later, her mother came downstairs to find the wine had overflowed the jug. Amity sat weeping on a low bench, her feet soaked.

"That ax," sobbed Amity, "it is so desperately sad."

"What of it?"

"One day, Blunt and I might marry. We might have a son, and we might name him Dingleberry."

"No, not Dingleberry. Boysenberry," said the mother.

"We might name him Dingleberry or Boysen-berry," said Amity, "and we would love him more than earth and sky. Dingleberry or Boysenberry might grow big, and soon he would be big enough to fetch wine from the cellar."

"Oh, what a big, strong boy!"

"Yes. We will be so proud of him. And Dingleberry or Boysenberry might come down here, and that ax, that ax! It might fall from its hook and cut the head clean off our big, strong boy."

"He'll never grow up to find true love," moaned the mother.

"We'll miss him so," said Amity, and she scooched over on the bench so the two of them could weep together.

Ten minutes later, the father came downstairs to find wine still pouring from the tap, soaking their feet and ankles.

"That ax," sobbed Amity, "it is so desperately sad."

"What of it?"

"One day, Blunt and I might marry. We might have a son, and we might name him Dingleberry or Boysenberry."

"Not Dingleberry or Boysenberry," said the father. "Brick."

"We might name him Dingleberry, Boysenberry, or Brick. And we would love him more than earth and sky." And so on Amity went, telling the story, and soon her father, too, was in tears.

"He'll never grow up to have children of his own," cried the father.

"He'll never grow up to find true love," cried the mother.

"We'll miss him so," said Amity.

Ten minutes later, Blunt came downstairs to find all three sitting on the low bench, weeping. The wine still poured from the tap and by now had soaked their legs up to the knees.

Blunt sloshed through the wine to the nearly empty cask. He turned it off. Then he found a bucket hanging on the wall and went to work tossing wine out the cellar door. When that was done, he dried the floor thoroughly.

"What's wrong?" he finally asked.

"That ax," sobbed Amity, "it is so desperately sad."

"What of it?"

"One day, you and I might marry. We might have a son, and we might name him Dingleberry, Boysenberry, or Brick." She told the whole story, weeping all the while, and when she had finished, Blunt stepped over to the ax. He took it off the hook and set it safely on the floor.

"I love you," said Blunt to Amity, "but we cannot get married."

"Why not?"

"You and your parents are three of the greatest noodles I ever saw. Wasting all that wine. Ruining your clothes. Making a mess of the cellar and weeping over an ax you can move with no trouble at all. Worrying about a son we haven't got, and giving him ridiculous names. I can't live my life among noodles!" cried Blunt.

"But there are noodles everywhere," said Amity. "You won't be free of noodles, whatever you do."

"I will go on a journey," said Blunt. "And if on my travels, I find three greater noodles than you, then all right. I'll come back and marry into this noodley family."

"Well, then, I'll see you in a week or two," said Amity.

"I doubt it," said Blunt. But he gave her a kiss before he left.

BLUNT TRAVELED on horseback. He had only been gone a day when he came across an old woman, hobbling along with a sieve held carefully in front of her.

"What are you doing?" he asked.

"What does it look like I'm doing? I'm fetching water from the village well."

"You don't do it like that."

"Yes, I do."

"No, you don't."

"Yes, I do."

"All the water pours through the holes in the sieve," Blunt explained. "Look, you've almost none left. Let me give you a jug."

"What a know-it-all you are," said the old woman. "Look at me. I'm near to eighty years old, and I've been fetching water this way since I was born. Take your jug and be off."

"Aren't you thirsty?"

"Get on away from me," she said. "Smarty know-it-all."

So off Blunt went, bidding her good day and good luck.

That was one great noodle, and a cranky one, too.

THAT NIGHT, Blunt stopped at an inn. It was so full of customers that he had to share a room with another fellow. When he awoke, he found that his roommate, an old gentleman with long whiskers, had hung his trousers on the knobs of the dresser. Blunt watched as the man climbed onto a chair and jumped.

Whoomp! He fell to the floor.

"Are you all right?" Blunt helped the old man to his feet.

"Let me alone to put me trousers on," said the gentleman. Ignoring his bleeding knee, he climbed on the chair again.

Whoomp! He fell to the floor again.

"You don't put your trousers on that way," said Blunt.

"Yes, I do."

"No, you don't."

"Yes, I do."

"You sit on the chair and put them on one leg at a time, like so." Blunt demonstrated with his own trousers.

"What a know-it-all you are," said the old gentleman. "Look at me. I'm near to eighty years old, and I've been putting me trousers on this way since I was born."

"But you're bleeding."

"Hmph."

"And it takes so long."

"Only about an hour. Now get on away from me. Smarty know-it-all."

The old gentleman was climbing back on the chair and preparing to jump again when Blunt left the room.

So that was the second great noodle, and a mean one, too.

BLUNT RODE ALL DAY, and as night fell, he came to a pond just outside a small town where he hoped to spend the night. There was a crowd of men and women around the pond, each holding a rake.

"What are you doing?" asked Blunt.

"What does it look like we're doing?" one of the men answered. "The moon has fallen into the pond, and we're trying to get her out."

"But it's not in the pond."

"Yes, it is."

"No, it isn't."

"Yes, it is."

"The moon is in the sky like always," explained Blunt. "What you see in the pond is only her reflection."

"What a know-it-all you are," said the man. "What makes you think you understand more than all us people?" And with that, he ran at Blunt, waving his rake. "Get on away from here," he cried. "Smarty know-it-all."

Several of the others followed, waving their rakes and yelling.

Blunt and his horse ran away as fast as they could.

So that was a whole number of great noodles, and violent ones, too.

SEEING THE MOON so full above him reminded

Blunt of Amity. The two of them used to stroll in the evenings by the light of that same moon.

Maybe she was looking at it now and thinking of him?

There were indeed so many great noodles in the world, thought Blunt. Those he'd met on this journey were cranky. They were mean and violent.

Blunt felt quite lucky, suddenly, to have found a future wife so tenderhearted as Amity, noodle though she was.

He loved her, and so he went home.

"You've only been gone three days," said Amity, planting a kiss on his cheek. "Did you find three great noodles?"

"Many more than three great noodles," said Blunt.

"I told you so," said she.

"What a know-it-all you are," he said. "Shall we get married, then?"

"We should, indeed," said she.

And that is what they did, and, to be sure, it worked out very well.

Hansel
and
Gretel

THERE WERE ONCE two children, a boy and a girl, whose mother died. They lived in a little brick house with a smoking chimney, and their names were Hansel and Gretel. After their mother's death, they were mournful and sometimes lonely, but they did not turn bitter. They found joy in one another's company, the warm taste of chocolate, the sweet sharpness of peppermint, and the sour brightness of lemon drops.

Their father was a woodcutter, and he was so sad at losing his wife that he could not be consoled by the sweetness of candy nor the smiles of children. He became stupid with grief, even stupider than other stupid, grieving people. He felt the world was cruel, and he was far too unhappy to make dinner, cut wood, do his accounts, or even think like a reasonable person.

One day, he found a woman who would do all those things for him. He married her as quickly as possible.

This stepmother, she cut wood and sold wood, made dinner, did the accounts, and even thought like a reasonable person, none of which was easy.

Why did she marry him when she did all the work and he did nothing? Well, she was no longer young, and the woodcutter was exceedingly handsome, to most people's way of thinking. Good looks can make people giddy sometimes.

Anyway, the stepmother's days were hard and long, much harder and longer than she ever thought they'd be. Quite quickly she saw that feeding two hungry children every day — especially two with a taste for chocolate, peppermint, and lemon drops — feeding them was not a reasonable thing for a hardworking woman to do.

Nearby, there was a forest; a strange and frozen

forest you may have heard about before. The animals who lived there were very, very hungry, and the weather so cold, it would kill a person in a few days, if the animals didn't get him first.

The stepmother told the father a plan she had devised. She proposed to lose the children in the frozen forest.

Their father, in the stupid way of people lost in their own grief, did not argue. He was grateful for all her hard work. He was afraid she would leave him.

Hansel and Gretel overheard the conversation, and, that evening, Hansel gathered two pocketsful of the bright yellow pebbles that lined the cottage path.

When the stepmother took the children into the frozen forest on the premise of fresh air and exercise, Hansel dropped the pebbles as they walked on the snowy path.

The stepmother turned right, then left. Crossed a frozen stream on a fallen tree. Turned left, then right.

When she left them in the depth of the winter forest, running away on long legs so fast the children couldn't possibly catch her, Hansel and Gretel held hands and followed the bright yellow pebbles home.

Their father welcomed them with a feeble smile.

Their stepmother did not.

After that they lived together as they had done before, but the woodcutting was still hard, and the dinners were sparse. The accounts were still tricky, and since the father was still stupid with grief over his previous wife, the stepmother became even more reasonable than she had been before.

This time, when she took the children into the forest, she did not discuss it with anyone beforehand. Hansel had no time to gather bright yellow pebbles. All he had to mark the way home was a heel of bread in his pocket. This he crumbled and dropped as the three of them walked the twisted, icy paths. "Don't worry, Gretel," he whispered. "The crumbs will guide our way home."

"We don't need them," said Gretel.

"Why not?"

"I don't want to go back to that house again," she said. "Nobody there loves me enough to save me from this frozen forest."

"I love you enough," said Hansel.

"You will be in the forest with me," Gretel said. "And so that means I'll be home already."

Still Hansel dropped his crumbs, intending to find his way out. If they did not go home to their father and stepmother, then at least they would search out somewhere warm to sleep the night.

When their stepmother left them in the depth of the forest, again running away on long legs so fast the children couldn't possibly catch her, Hansel and Gretel held hands and looked for the bread crumbs to lead them out.

They were not there.

After all, the animals who lived in that forest were very, very hungry. Those crumbs had been snatched up by ravens almost as soon as Hansel had dropped them.

As night fell, Hansel and Gretel wandered the twisted paths of ice and snow. Luck was not with them. Yellow eyes looked at them from bare trees and bushes. Eyes of wolves and foxes who were starving for meat. Eyes of vultures, ravens, and owls who were starving likewise. Eyes of bears.

At last, the shivering children saw a warm glow through the dark. They followed the light. Soon the iced path became a walkway of what looked like bright yellow pebbles, and they stepped into a clearing marked off with a neat wooden fence.

Inside the fence, no starving animals lurked. It was warm. The smell of gingerbread filled the air. At the center of the clearing stood a sugar house.

The walkway wasn't made of yellow pebbles but of lemon drops, sour and bright. The bricks were made of gingerbread cake, and the mortar, chocolate. Smoke rose from the chimney. The doorway of the house was rimmed round with sweet, sharp peppermints, and the windows with black licorice. The snow that capped the roof and windows was not snow but frosting, smelling of vanilla.

It was the most beautiful home they had ever seen.

Hansel and Gretel were so hungry they began to eat at once, but they had only just filled their mouths when they heard a voice.

Nibble, nibble,
Little, little;

Thin, too thin,
You must come in.

With chocolate smearing their faces and gingerbread on their tongues, Hansel and Gretel looked up to see an old woman, blind as could be, standing in the open doorway. She repeated:

Nibble, nibble,
Little, little;
Thin, too thin,
You must come in.

The children went in. They never should have. But who can blame them? They were stupid with cold and hunger and loneliness. They did not even wonder how the woman knew they were thin when she was blind; and they did not wonder why she wasn't angry that they had eaten her sugar house.

The woman fed them candied nuts and pancakes with syrup, hot chocolate and pumpkin pie. "How did you come to wander here?" she asked.

They told her of their useless father and their

terrifyingly reasonable stepmother. She made kind noises and asked them their names. When they asked hers, she replied, "You can call me Old Mother."

They were glad enough to do so. Who wouldn't want an Old Mother and a sugar house, when nobody loved them enough at home?

They went to sleep under thick blankets, but when Gretel woke in the morning, Hansel was not beside her.

She threw off the covers and ran downstairs.

There was Old Mother, stirring a pot of steaming chocolate on the stove. And there was Hansel, trapped in a large cage that now hung from the kitchen ceiling.

"I'm fattening him up," said Old Mother. "Don't cry. You didn't imagine I fed you for nothing, did you? Fed you from the kindness of my heart?"

Gretel had thought exactly that. Of course she had. "Why did you feed us, then?"

"I feed you, my luscious children, in order to feed myself," said Old Mother. "And when the boy is fat and squashy like a sausage, I shall have my supper."

"You can't do this!" Gretel ran to the cage and

shook it, looking for a door or a latch — but there was none. "I won't let her hurt you," she told Hansel. "I won't. I'll get help. I'll come back and get you out."

But Old Mother snatched her arm. She could not see Gretel, but she could smell her the way anyone hungry smells meat. "No one finds this sugar house unless I let them find it," she said. "And lost in this forest, you'll die of cold or be eaten alive."

Gretel shook her arm hard, trying to release the old woman's grip, but Hansel's voice stopped her.

"Don't leave me," he said. "Please, don't leave me."

He was her only true family.

Gretel did not leave.

OVER THE COMING WEEKS, Old Mother fattened Hansel for the enormous hot oven that stood in one corner of her kitchen. "I'll char you like a marshmallow," she told him, "and eat your soft sweet insides." She fed him on lemon drops and pound cakes, gingerbreads and hot chocolate, pushing the food through the narrow bars of the cage and repeating:

Nibble, nibble,
Little, little;
Eat, now eat,
My lovely meat.

Each day she demanded Hansel let her squeeze his finger. "When your fingers are fat and squashy is when I'll have you," she told him. "Chubby boys are hard to come by in this frozen forest."

But Hansel was no noodle, and though he did eat all the goodies and grew fat, he had found an old bone on the floor of his cage. It was the bone he poked through for the blind witch to squeeze, and so it seemed to her, day after day, that he remained too thin to make a good meal.

Old Mother scolded Gretel. She hit her and told her she was worthless. She made Gretel scrub the floors and wash the windows, beat the carpets and cook the meals. Old Mother made her do the dishes, wash the clothes, make the beds, and mend the holes in her stockings.

Each day, Gretel searched for a way to open Hansel's cage. But each day, she failed.

One morning, as they sat in the kitchen eating chocolate cake and clotted cream, Old Mother reached across the table and grabbed Gretel's hand. She squeezed Gretel's now-plump fingers, one by one. "If not the one, then the other," she muttered to herself. "My appetite for meat can wait no more."

Then aloud, she said: "Gretel, check the oven to see if it is hot yet. I want to bake that strudel your brother likes so much."

But Gretel was no noodle, either. She knew full well what it meant that Old Mother had squeezed her fingers. If she did not think fast, she would soon be charred like a marshmallow herself.

"Pardon me, Old Mother?"

"Lean into the oven and feel if it is hot yet," repeated the witch.

"I do not understand, Old Mother. Will you show me?"

"Do like so!" snapped the witch. She marched to the oven, opened the heavy door, and leaned into it. "Feel if it is hot yet, worthless girl."

Gretel saw her chance. She threw herself on Old Mother and pushed her into the hot fires of the oven.

Then she shut the heavy iron door and bolted it tight. And listened.

She heard curses.

Banging.

Screams.

And silence.

Gretel stood and watched the door of the oven, fearing Old Mother might come out of it at any moment.

She did not.

Suddenly, the walls of Hansel's cage opened of their own accord. "She is dead, then," he said, reaching for his sister's hand.

They armed themselves with knives from the kitchen drawers. They filled bags and pockets with peppermints, chocolate, and lemon drops. They pulled bricks of gingerbread from the walls and carried them to feed the hungry animals of the wintery forest. They wrapped themselves in blankets and left the sugar house, empty, with smoke still rising from the chimney.

CRUEL YELLOW EYES looked at them from the shadows. They fed the wolves and bears on gingerbread. Dark wings flapped overhead, and they fed the ravens likewise. Finally, after many hours, Hansel and Gretel walked out of the woods onto a green hillside. There was a rush of warm air on their faces, and they squinted in the sunshine.

Down the hill, they could see their father's house. The chimney smoked merrily.

"I am not sure I want to go back to that house again," said Gretel. "Nobody there loves me enough to save me from the frozen forest."

"I love you enough," said Hansel.

"If you will be in the house with me," said Gretel, "it will be home no matter what else is wrong there."

"I think Stepmother is dead," said Hansel.

"You do?"

"Old Mother and Stepmother, too," said Hansel. "I am mostly certain."

And, indeed, he was right.

Hansel and Gretel's father heard their steps on the yellow pebbles that lined the cottage path. He ran out of the house to embrace them, a face full of tears and a mouth full of regrets.

He took them inside and made them dinner.

They warmed their hands at the fire and drank hot milk.

All evening, the three of them talked and ate and cried. Anger and shame, forgiveness and promises.

It was not easy. But it was family.

The little brick house with the smoking chimney was once again a home.

AUTHOR'S NOTE

My attempt here was not to be accurate to any previous versions of these tales. I am not retelling these stories to demonstrate the breadth or care of my research. At the same time, I am not reinventing the tales. Were I reinventing, I might have jacked up the stories with new contexts, antics, and details, the way movies like *Tangled* and *Puss in Boots* do. Or I might have rewritten them with feminist or satirical endings so as to critique the originals.

What I'm doing instead is telling these stories largely faithfully, but without adhering to versions made famous by Charles Perrault, the Brothers Grimm, and others. I wrote them simply as I myself want to tell them, using the storytelling techniques I have at my disposal. After all, before people began writing them down, these tales were passed down orally. They changed a bit with each new teller. I wrote to bring out what's most meaningful to me in the stories, and in that way I believe I am part of a tradition that goes back to the earliest tellers of these tales.

As I wrote, I searched for answers to questions. Why would Red trust the wolf? How would it feel to have pearls dropping from your mouth? Why would an enchanted frog love a selfish princess, or a smart man marry a silly woman? Why is Hansel and Gretel's cruel stepmother dead upon their return?

I grew up with picture book fairy tales illustrated by Paul Galdone, Trina Schart Hyman, and the artists of the Walt Disney Company. Later I graduated to reading the famous collections by Andrew Lang and Howard Pyle, as well as Perrault and the Brothers Grimm. I still have my copies of the Lang and Pyle collections, their paperback bindings so worn that some of them are held together with rubber bands.

In graduate school, where I wrote a dissertation on the illustrated novels of the late nineteenth and early twentieth centuries, I collected books of fairy tales illustrated by Walter Crane, Harry Clarke, Arthur Rackham, Kay Neilsen, and the like. These stories have followed me into adulthood, and I am now very glad to share my versions of them with you.